THE GIRAFFE
WHO WENT TO SCHOOL

This is my

WONDER® BOOK

. . . .

THE GIRAFFE
WHO WENT TO SCHOOL

Story and pictures

by **IRMA WILDE**

Wonder® Books
PRICE/STERN/SLOAN
Publishers, Inc., Los Angeles
1986

Copyright© 1951 by Price/Stern/Sloan Publishers, Inc.
Published by Price/Stern/Sloan Publishers, Inc.
410 North La Cienega Boulevard, Los Angeles, California 90048

ISBN: 0-8431-4104-2

Wonder® Books is a trademark of Price/Stern/Sloan Publishers, Inc.

IN A BIG old-fashioned house, two ladies had a school where they taught four little girls.

The ladies' names were Miss Bee and Miss Dee.

The four little girls were Mary, Ann, Nancy and Pam.
They learned how to read and write and sew.

They learned to sing and dance.

They had French lessons too, and were taught to say, "Pardonnez-moi," which means "Pardon me," and "S'il vous plait," which means "If you please."
Everyone thought the children had lovely manners.

Now, down the road from Miss Bee and Miss Dee's school was a small zoo, where Alice the tame giraffe lived. Every day she would stretch her long neck out as far as it would go – which was pretty far – and look over to where Mary, Ann, Nancy and Pam were playing games and reading books under the big trees in the yard.

"Oh, if I could only go to school, too," sighed Alice. "I would be so good and study so hard. Oh, I wish I could go to school!"

So one day she got up very early, walked out the front
gate, down the road, and followed Mary, Ann, Nancy and
Pam right up to the schoolhouse.

Miss Bee and Miss Dee were rather surprised, for they
had never had a giraffe to teach before.

"Please, please, Miss Bee," said Mary and Ann. "Please let Alice stay."

"Please, please, Miss Dee," said Nancy and Pam. "Please let Alice stay."

So Miss Bee and Miss Dee said they would be delighted to have Alice in their school.

"Now we will all stand up straight and tall and sing 'America,'" said Miss Bee. Alice held her head up high like the children, but – OUCH – it bumped the ceiling!

"Now we will all sit in a circle and read," said Miss Dee.

Alice tried and tried, but she simply couldn't get comfortable in her little chair. And as for reading — well, big as she was, Alice just couldn't learn her A B C's.

"We are so sorry," said Miss Bee and Miss Dee, "but Alice will have to go back to her own home at the zoo."

"Then she won't be here tomorrow for May Day and dance around the Maypole with us," cried Mary, Ann, Nancy and Pam. "Oh dear, oh dear!" Everyone was sad. Alice was the saddest of all as she went home to the zoo.

Big tears fell down her cheeks the next day when she stretched her neck out and saw the children gathered around the Maypole. They looked lovely and she wanted so much to be with them instead of just looking on.

Suddenly a little breeze started to blow, and it blew and blew and blew itself into a great big wind.

It blew the four little girls' hair ribbons and sashes. And it blew Miss Bee's frilly blouse. And it blew Miss Dee's ruffles on her skirt.

Worst of all, it blew the Maypole right out of the ground, up into the air, and out of sight over the treetops.

So the wind went away with the Maypole. What a dreadful thing to happen! Who ever heard of a May Day without a Maypole? And what in the world were they to do? Miss Bee was distressed, and Miss Dee was distracted, and Mary, Ann, Nancy and Pam were so disappointed that they cried.

But Alice had been watching everything right from the zoo. "I wonder," thought Alice. "Could I help? I wonder – maybe I could! I wonder – yes, I'll do it!"

She raced down the road. She ran into the garden.

"Quick," said Alice to Miss Dee, "get more flowers."

"Quick, quick," said Alice to Miss Bee, "Get more
ribbons."

"Quick, quick, quick," said Alice to the children. "Fasten them on my head. *I* will be your Maypole!"

So Mary, Ann, Nancy and Pam danced around Alice and sang their May Day songs.

They sang and sang, and danced and danced, and it was the best May Day Mary, Ann, Nancy and Pam ever had.

"And Alice is the best Maypole we have ever had," Miss Bee and Miss Dee agreed.

"Even if Alice can't read and count and play games, she can be the most beautiful Maypole in the world," said Mary, Ann, Nancy and Pam.

This made Alice very, very happy. She thought it was the very best thing anyone had ever said about her, and after this wonderful day she knew she would always be happy in her home at the zoo.